ALL WF

CHORLEY
Creative Writing Festival

3rd May – 26th July 2003

Featuring

Janice Connolly 'Holy Mary' from Phoenix Nights
Jim Bennett Liverpool's 'Voice of Culture'
Caroline Gilfillan Prize Winning Poet
Alison Chisholm from Writer's News
Margaret Murphy from the Murder Squad
Helen Eatock T.V. Scriptwriter
Vera Waters Life Coach
Jane Eagland, Children's Writer
Dianne Darby from the Text Factory
Julie Meadows Healer and Writer
Geoff Dixon from MMOR Music
Anne Caldwell Reading Addict

Presented by Chorley & District Writers Circle

MOLE PRESS
Whitstable, KENT

ISBN 1 898030 07 7

Copyright 2003 Mole Press

British Library Cataloguing in Publication Data available.

Cover Design by Glenda Charlesworth & Liz Perry

Printed in Kent by JRDigital Print Services Ltd

CONTENTS

FOREWORD
by Jim Bennett

Brilliant! That is the only word for it. All of it absolutely brilliant; the organisation, the effort from those participating and the general feeling of people striving to create.

I must admit to some misgivings as the programme of events landed on the doorstep. It seemed very ambitious and you couldn't help but feel that maybe the organisers were over-reaching themselves with a festival lasting for twelve weeks and covering fifteen individual workshops and a final theatre performance, especially as this was to be the first festival of its kind in Chorley.

I was down to open the festival with a workshop which was an introduction to Creative Writing. I need not have worried, as soon as I turned up for my session I was met with an eagerness and energy from the participants which was astounding and it was clear then that the festival would be a success.

My next contact with the festival was to be 12 weeks later when I was invited to be part of the closing night performance at the Little Theatre in Chorley. Although several of those appearing on stage that night had some experience of reading or performing their work previously, many had never appeared on a stage or read in public anywhere before, but you would never have known. What a fabulous night it was.

If anyone were to ask me if the first Chorley Creative Writing Festival was a success then I would tell them of the people who had never written anything before, but who came wanting to, and how when they had taken those first steps they went on to perform those words, entertaining an appreciative audience weeks later. But anything I say will

1

be insignificant next to the personal success stories which could be told by many of those who found they had a voice and a means to have it heard for the first time.

If anyone wants to know if the first Chorley Festival of Literature was a success then I would just direct them to this anthology and let the writers speak for themselves.

Jim Bennett

Jim Bennett is the editor of The Poetry Kit Magazine and the author of 54 books. He delivers courses on creative writing for The University of Liverpool, Edge Hill University College and the WEA.

ON TO THE PAGE

First Steps in Creative Writing
With Jim Bennett

The Festival opened on Saturday 3rd May with 'On To The Page', a workshop designed to be a guide for beginners to creative writing of all genres. The tutor was Jim Bennett who is well known in his native Liverpool as a performance poet, song writer and script writer. One of Jim's main tips was to have a notebook and pencil at all times, even tucked away under the pillow to record ideas thoughts and snips of conversations.

We were given suggestions for constructing and setting out pieces of work, all building up to a first draft which could then be altered or changed for better effect. Each person produced work on the day including a poem which was meant to convey in words sight, sound and smell.

Everyone who attended thoroughly enjoyed it and was encouraged to "have a go." The criticisms were both helpful and constructive.

Hazel Ratcliffe

HOME
by Susan Lane

When I think of home
I see glistening dark furniture urgently
polished
Along with plumped cushions and
well tended linen.

When I think of home
I hear the mumblings of Dad as the
Hoover goes on yet again.
Mum telling us off for getting dirty
amid wails of, "Where's my tea?"

When I think of home
I smell polish liberally sprayed
mingled along with cigarette smoke,
and oh those wonderful pies.

Susan Lane likes the simple life of going for a swim, taking a ride to the coast to watch the sea and walking in the park.

CHILDHOOD
by Hazel Ratcliffe

When I think of childhood
I hear the sound of clogs and work boots clattering over
the cobbled streets.
Terraced houses whose occupants had been there
forever.
Slagheaps, last remnants of abandoned, water filled
collieries.
Neighbours chatting on doorsteps, small corner shops
and donkey stones.

When I think of childhood
I remember listening to Children's Favourites on an old
battered wireless.
Sitting at a school desk chanting times tables over and
over again, now locked into the brain for perpetuity.
My Mother standing at the door calling my name in a less
than stage whisper.
The sound of birds singing as we gathered blackberries
in the hedgerows.

When I think of childhood
How could I forget the appetising aroma of freshly baked
cakes and homemade treacle toffee on bonfire night?
Beef stew with fluffy, plump dumplings, ripe juicy summer
strawberries.
Dolly tubs, mangles, washing hung outside and smelling
deliciously of fresh air.

Hazel Ratcliffe started writing poetry when she retired
from her job in a Building Society. The majority of her
poems contain some humour, past personal experiences
and nostalgia. Her other hobbies include the theatre,
singing and guitar lessons.

IRELAND
by Pauline Hayden

When I think of Ireland
I think of leisure.
The friendliness of people
and feeling spiritually better
for having been taken away
from the stress and strain
of modern living for one glorious week.
The smell of the turf fire burning.
The leisurely breakfasts
and the smell of fresh mown hay
a joy to the senses.
The jolly conversation
the music played, the hymn singing
and the serious sermon.
All blend together
with the places we have visited
and the characters we have encountered
upon the way.

Pauline Hayden enjoys the quiet side of life; embroidery, Irish music and holidays associated with historical interest.

MEMORIES

by Irene Greenall

I remember the lounge in my parent's house.
My Mother playing the piano and friends gathered around.
The ornate music glass fronted cabinet in the corner.
The glowing coal fire, antique ornaments chosen with great care and the silver tray set with delicate china in preparation for afternoon tea, but most of all the atmosphere of love and joy. Glances passing between my Mother and Father like electric sparks.
The scent of Mother's perfume and the flowers. The pink hawthorn tree in bloom, its delicate smell wafting in through the open window mingling with the newly mown lawn.
The aroma of hot coffee and cakes baked to perfection.
The tuneful melodies brilliantly played by Mother on the piano. The sounds of laughter and fun. Friends singing with great enthusiasm.
My Father's hand on Mother's shoulder as he sang love songs to her.
I remember the reaction of people who entered. They would remark that there was a unique atmosphere of warmth, comfort and welcome.
It was as if the bricks had absorbed the joy, love and happiness that had gone before.
It was magical. Music seemed more brilliant, the aroma of flowers more perfumed, the rooms more attractive.
It was as if an invisible presence had entered and waved a wand of ambiance.
I shall remember it forever.

THE MOMENT OF TRUTH
by Irene Greenall

It had been a terrible day, the 'phone call was garbled and almost unintelligible. He must get home as quickly as possible. What had happened? Had there been an accident, and to whom? Was someone ill? His wife, children? The possibilities were endless. The voice he had heard was agitated with mumbled sentences which did not fully convey what had happened.

Panic set in as he was driving a little erratically. His home was in the distance and everything took on an unreal air. His hands trembled as the key was put into the lock and a feeling of nausea overtook him. His legs crumpled beneath him.

Everything was quiet with an air of normality. The door beyond beckoned. He felt loath to enter for his whole life, success, wealth, love and family, all his striving could change in an instant. Once again sheer blind panic assailed him. His heart was thumping; thump, thump, thump – this was the moment of truth......

Ten years ago **Irene Greenall** ventured into writing poetry and has had poems published in 65 books, plus a number for the International Library of Poetry based in America. She has had five Editor's Choice Awards and been invited to America on a number of occasions. Irene donated a poem entitled "The War to End all Wars" which pays homage to the veterans of the First World War. This poem has been placed on the window ledge of the Room of Remembrance in Astley Hall. Irene joined Chorley Writers' Circle at its inception.

8

THE DOUBLE DOORS
by Christine McGlynn

Bernard glanced up at the large clock on the opposite wall. With trembling hands he took the letter from his inside jacket pocket, slowly unfolded it, muttering the words to himself as he read it. He re-folded it and carefully replaced it in his well-worn leather wallet. He held the wallet for a moment, turning it over in his hands, before returning it to the security of his inside pocket.

Once more he glanced up at the big wall-clock, before reaching forward to the table strewn with an assortment of magazines. He hesitated, then selected the one nearest to him, and sat back with it unopened on his knee.

Just as he began to turn the pages, his name was called, but as he reached to collect his raincoat from the next chair, the un-read magazine slipped to the floor. Clumsily, he stretched down for it, and almost threw it back on the table. As he straightened himself, he took a deep breath before walking slowly towards the double doors.

A FAVOURITE PLACE
by Christine McGlynn

It wasn't the sight of the clean, clear water tumbling over the rocks, or the twisting, climbing gravel roads that went on for miles without signs of habitation that made my first visit to that forest in Scotland so memorable. It was the sight of that vast green ocean of gently swaying treetops, that stretched in all directions, as far as the eye could see.

Neither did the sound of bird-song, the whispering trees and snapping twigs, or the incessant bubbling and swishing of the streams make the most lasting impression on my senses. The sound I associate most with the forest, that I could listen to for hours, is the elusive, yet almost tangible sound of the all encompassing silence.

Christine McGlynn is now retired, but has been a junior and infant teacher, and more recently spent several years running a picture-framing business with her husband. She has always wanted to write, but is only now finding the time to get some of her ideas down on paper. She has written several short stories, as yet unpublished, and is half-way through writing her first novel.

TABLE MOUNTAIN
by Blythe Jones

When I think of Table Mountain,
I remember the jagged, tree-covered edges rising in front
of me.
The flat table top, stark against the blue sky.
The white clouds tumbling freely over the edge, falling
towards me.

When I think of Table Mountain,
I remember the smell of freshly cut lawn as I leave the
manicured botanical gardens behind me.
The scent of pine, of rotting vegetation.
The fresh air, free from the pollutions of city life.

When I think of Table Mountain,
I remember hearing the rustle of the undergrowth.
The noise of my footsteps as I stumble over small rocks
and unearth loose stones,
and shiver against the chill of the cold wind rustling the
leaves in the forest below.

When I think of Table Mountain, I think of home.

Blythe Jones aspires to be a great writer - if only she
could discipline herself. She dreams of Africa but is in
love with a certain Brit, which keeps her here. She also
loves Frank Sinatra, fine red wine, and her beloved dog,
Charlie.

ABSTRACTION

Experimentation
With Dianne Darby

This workshop was quite different to the usual type of Creative Writing workshop and dealt solely with stimulating the imagination. We began by examining and selecting abstract pictures or postcards and writing lists of words which sprang to mind. We then exchanged the lists and each composed a poem using just the words on those lists.

The second exercise was similar, but this time we used interesting scenes and photographs, composing words from our own list this time. Everyone was most enthusiastic and some interesting and surprising work came from these methods, which allowed free rein to imagination and engendered much lively discussion and laughter.

In the afternoon we listened to sound, at the same time conjuring up images, shapes, emotions and colours. One member had a wonderful wacky time and drew amazing shapes in coloured pens. One tip we were given was to use unlined paper so that the lines did not inhibit expression of ideas. Brilliant workshop and quite out of the ordinary.

Gwen Weiss

Dianne Darby is a poet and fiction writer whose first collection, *Perfect Legs*, a combination of poetry and short stories, was published in 1995. She has run many writing workshops in both poetry and prose, mostly at the Text Factory in Yorkshire.

DISCORDANT MUSIC
by Gwen Weiss

Motorway clamour instils vague fear,
draws near then fades.
A splash sets things in motion.
Metal tubes clatter clatter clang;
Tiny mice feet patter,
marbles roll across the floor,
diminish, disappear.
Heavy hammers beat a rhythm.
I dance, arms outstretched.
I'm orange and red.
I climb, fly high;
I fall.
Someone's there;
My shallow breath leaves me hollow.
Crash! Broken glass, shards splinter tinkle
scatter tinkle.
I gasp.
Knives sharp, steel grey flash and twist.
Voices!
I am not alone.

Peaceful now,
bathed in pale blue
I languish on soft cushions
amid while floaty curtains.
I am at rest.

DRAGONLAND
by Gwen Weiss

Valleys, mountains,
Highlands, uplands
Tucked and puckered,
formed, deformed.
Gaia's heaving bosom.

Earth child exposed semi naked,
Only weapons – sticks and stones
Scaly shiny dragon-lizard
Scarred and hungry, overgrown.
Flashes blazing flame;

Victim screams in pain and terror;
Brothers gaze in fascination,
cannot comprehend the horror.
at the sickening transformation:
Scorched flesh stink.

Smooth sleek skin layers stripped,
blistered, seared, red and raw,
grainy crusted corrugated
only inches from the open maw's
dreadful teeth.

A mountain top rends asunder,
Hurling rocks in its turn.
A crack reverberates like thunder.
Now it's the dragon's time to burn.
He flees and dies.

Others run to injured brother,
carry him to sheltering cave.
Merest touch gives searing pain

He clenches teeth; he must be brave.
They tend with herbs.

The wounds are healed, they're celebrating
but his mind can't find relief.
Each day relives that primal terror
That brush with death, so close, so brief.
A lifelong horror.

This man is crushed!

IN OPPOSITION
by Gwen Weiss

Wholesome, healthy,
Mushroom omelette and brown bread.
Hungry, tasty, aroma.
Evocative, sensual, cuddlybum!
Desire, oneness.
Constraining, dead, buried.

Varicosed legs in laddered stockings.
Walking stick.
Suffering.
Blood, dripping upwards, choking.
Silent.
Death.
God???

Gwen Weiss is a retired midwife. She is the driving force behind Writer's Inc and also a member of Preston Poets and Chorley Writer's Circle as well as two reading groups. Gwen has had numerous poems published in anthologies and magazines.

BEACHSCAPE WITH MODEL
by Jackie Hayes

Archways.
Moon, white, ethereal idles.
Blurs focus.
Warm skin, copper-gold beads.
Brown back, clasped hand, red nails.
Grains of sand.
Electric.

Interference. Power. Wealth.
Blue-folded note. Burnt.
Letters wound, cause conflict.
Vision tarnished.

MENACE
by Jackie Hayes

They came by night.
Menace was their name.
Where were they from?
Who could say.
Where were they bound?
Who could know.
Power is their driving-force
and they are fuelled by lust.
They are clothed in darkness
and sound-bursts are their heralds.
Their passing vibrates all the earth,
their footsteps shake the air.
All creatures cower at their coming.

who can discern their purpose?
Trees tremble at their passing,
buds break beneath their tread.

And in their wake the dancers came...
yet not the carefree revels of the spring
or joyous frolic to bring in the may
These dancers have a purpose sharp and clear,
no less a threat than all the warrior band.
Their trumpet's brassy strident note a sign
for ever powerful thrusting surge,
then instruments like glass splinter the air
with silver shivers, simmering the air,
trembling, turning, pirouetting, spinning,
the dancers twisting in the clamorous night.
Now saffron gong sets all to flitter,
and flickering, flitting, flowing with the tide
of swaying, surging singers, sounding
sonorous notes
they swelled to crimson climax as their thrusts
grew ever wilder.
And so they passed into the void beyond.

Jackie Hayes is a member of Preston Poets Society, Writers Inc., Lancashire Author's Association and is currently involved with a small group of poets who meet to workshop in Blackpool.

ABSTRACT LAKE
by Carol Thistlethwaite

Blue yellow tartan ripples across a loch
like pleats in Scottish reels.
Grey winds blow cold
voices through telegraph wires,
as black horses gallop, furrowing the surface.
Yellow winds blow warm
whispers whirl away grey leaves,
Indian bracelets, bronze and gold, dance
concentric rings echo out,
distorting memories in a pool
of smiling melodies.
Blue winds blow,
dancers twist and weave across the surface
spinning memories into thread,
echoes swing,
as memories breeze across the lake.

Carol Thistlethwaite is a graduate from Edge Hill university college where she is about to begin an MA in writing studies. Carol is a new writer who explores many forms including visual poetry; she is published in several anthologies, journals and magazines.

GUNMETAL MOON
by Liz Perry

A gunmetal moon
shadows a monochrome landscape,
rippling tranquillity's quiet tide
across the estuary.

Clouds drifting
signpost a silver promontory
against the moonlit skyline.
Black pools empty in silence.
Flowing into runnels,
channelling toward the flat horizon.

An eerie pewter sheen glimmers
in the dreamscape of this solitude.

Liz Perry keeps no cats or dogs, has no baggy cardigans or
fluffy slippers. She plans to live in a wild place, ride her bike, play
her music loud and grow old disgracefully!

GOBBLEDYGOOK
by Chris Collison

Yellow lime banana split
and cherry sauce to "bleed" on it.
Christmas tree has soft red balls,
smoke will splutter round the halls
and choke hobnobbers just a bit
where mouths are crude and full of shit.

WHAT'S YOUR POISON?

Crime Writing
With Margaret Murphy

This was a workshop where we spent quite a lot of time listening, in order to analyse portions of recorded material, studying how different authors had dealt with character building and setting. Then we discussed the different types of murder stories: classic, suspense, detective, noir fiction, thriller espionage, historical crime, and literary crime. We were shown examples of how to introduce characters, and how to integrate action and interior monologue with description and how we could develop our characters.

In the afternoon we had to choose a person from a whole selection of photographs and had to write a short piece on that person, as if we were introducing that person in a piece of writing. Finally we were given handouts of other courses, useful books and 'Murder Writing Festivals.' This was a quiet and thoughtful workshop but everyone said they had enjoyed it, and were sorry when it ended.

Gwen Weiss

Margaret Murphy is a member of 'The Murder Squad' and a successful crime writer. Her novels, Weaving Shadows, Darkness Falls, Past Reason and Dying Embers are available from Chorley library.

MAGGIE
by Brenda Stobie

Maggie didn't just sit at the end of the bar. She filled the space like a poisonous smoking volcano. Her eyes glowered at me from sockets set deeply into her thin sallow face. The manly shirt, the black trousers, almost asked me to comment on her butchness, surveying the closed door.

Her eyes never left my face as I slowly closed the space between us.

"Excuse me," my voice was too high, too apologetic, "would you be Maggie O'Farrel?"

"Might be. Depends who's asking."

Her accent had a mixture but there was definitely some Irish in there somewhere.

"My name is Meryl. I think we might be related."

Taking a long leisurely draw on her cigarette Maggie's ancient eyes looked me up and down and then she started a deep throaty smoker's laugh. I had waited 20 years for this moment. I was terrified what the next ten seconds would bring.

Brenda Stobie has retired from work but not from life. She paints a bit, gardens a bit, writes a bit, cooks a lot.

THE BOSS
by Val Roberts

His huge glasses flashed once, twice in the light from the office window. He leaned forward, resting his elbows on the desk.

"And so, having evaluated your action plan for the company," he tapped his finger on the folder, "I have to tell you Miss...?" he raised one eyebrow interrogatively...

"Jones," I supplied,

"Jones," he enunciated, carefully committing it to memory, "I am not at all happy with your suggestions for further expansion." He slammed the folder open, finger jutting at the page. "All this could be done much more economically. For example, point three, paragraph two, sub-section one (a) suggests employing five staff to complement the new computer system." His gaze flicked swiftly upward and pinioned me. "Do you think five are really necessary? Could we perhaps not manage sufficiently with three?"

"Em possibly..."

"Good!" he snapped the folder shut and slid it smoothly towards me. "I shall expect your revised report at nine tomorrow morning."

He stood up, nodded and with an outstretched arm indicated that I should leave.

GRANDMA
by Jean C Blakeley

She was an elderly lady with wistful eyes, a faraway expression on her heavily wrinkled face. The full lips slightly parted betrayed the sensuousness of a once beautiful woman. The soft chiffon scarf over a plain dress and thick gold chain around her neck indicated that she had perhaps once been a woman of some substance.

Instinctively she touched the gold chain as she stared at the photograph on the piano.

"Are you alright Gran?" asked Charlotte who had been quietly observing her grandmother.

"I was remembering the day I met your grandfather," she replied falling silent again. A smile slowly crept across the worn face as her claw-like hand gently caressed the photograph and the wistful look returned to her pale eyes.

ALICE

by Lynne Taylor

Despite her age Alice's hair still shone and cascaded in a waterfall of curls and her strong sweet smile could still be projected over a crowded room. She had both buried and divorced four husbands and it was rumoured she was looking for her fifth.

At the moment she sat in the corner of the library of the old people's home from where she would survey the room. Taking out her powder compact she spied over it waiting and watching. The routine had been the same for the last few weeks, but not today. Today things would be different.

Alice sat surreptitiously surveying the closed door. As soon as she saw the handle move slowly downwards she snapped her compact closed and replaced it in her handbag as she stood up and sailed across the room neatly intercepting Major Bracewell.

"Ah Major, how kind of you to offer me your arm," she declared as she blatantly escorted the major through the now open dining room door. And all this before Miss Cresswell had even stood up.

That'll spike the old cow Cresswell's guns, she thought with a happy smile.

SONYA

by Gwen Weiss

Sonya fixed me with her blue-eyed innocent stare emphasised by her white fur - trimmed parka which seemed to envelop her protectively.

Although beautiful and young, a closer look revealed frown lines and the beginning of crow's-feet. I decided she was older than I had at first thought. Her long hair peeped out from her hood, tumbling in a golden cascade over her pale flawless cheeks. Her lips, the lower one full but not quite pouting added to her beauty.

Conscious of the impact she made on everyone she walked towards me graceful as a panther. She held out her hand and took mine, her grip surprisingly strong.

"Thank-you for coming," she purred softly. Eyes that had appeared to hold humour suddenly seemed steely, almost hostile.

I nodded, smiled briefly then looked away. Abruptly she released my hand, turned her back to me, swaying seductively towards her seat beside the still handsome elderly gentleman beside her.

WHAT'S YOUR POISON?

I do a lot of writers' workshops in the course of a year, and I am constantly surprised and gratified by the enthusiasm of the participants.

The Chorley festival was no exception. From beginners to the stalwarts of local writers' groups, the 'What's Your Poison?' workshop showed a willingness to try out new ideas and a determination to improve their skills.

It's always a privilege to hear people read their work, and on this occasion it was a great pleasure, too. It's a testament to the creativity of those present that from a common starting point, and in such a short time, they produced such an exciting variety of writing.

Margaret Murphy: The Murder Squad

THE HEALING POWERS OF WRITING

With Julie Meadows

Julie Meadows led us through a series of exercises including learning to relax with music, using a piece that appeals personally; an emotional test for which she produced an enormous palette of coloured pens, the colours you choose being as important as the design you draw.

Utilising experiences of pain and hurt to add depth to your writing. How encouraging young offenders to write poetry increased their self esteem. Grounding our feelings by expressing them on paper. Writing letters to someone who has angered or hurt us and sealing it in an envelope before deciding whether to send it.

Glenda Charlesworth

SOAR
by Glenda Charlesworth

Relax, unwind,
Roam free.
Thoughts unbounded,
Unfettered mind
Creating me.

27

?
by Glenda Charlesworth

One question.
I dare not ask.
The answer haunts.
I'll never know.

BREATHE
by Liz Perry

Imagine . . . .
You're standing on ribs of solid sand,
washed by the rhythm of a swelling tide.

Breathe. . . . .
You melt; fade to transparent
as the salt air ebbs and flows,

Breathe . . . .
Where is this palest yellow strand,
softly shifting on the western wind?

Breathe deeper . . . .
It lives in the solitude of the soul,
on the hopes of those who dream.
It's where the gently arcing dunes,
hold close to the solid land.

Let go . . . .
Yet, they are forever bound,
to the constant changeling sea.

PAX VOBISCUM

(Peace be with you)
by Liz Perry

For years,
I paddled in pools of forgiveness,
Careful not to tread on shards of broken promises,
or remains of secrets that wouldn't die.
Denial slipped so easily from your lips.
The corners of your mouth would twist to accommodate the lie.
Your eyes would brazen it out, focussed somewhere above my head,
inside I'd silently cry.

That last year,
I paddled in pools of forgiveness,
thinking my clearest thoughts, making plans for my future.
Of your so-called love I could find no sign,
as daily, by turns, you raged and sulked.
I waited, under siege, barricaded within, marking time.
My eyes would brazen it out, focussed somewhere above your head,
for I knew, peace would be mine.

amen

THE HEALING POWERS OF WRITING
by Julie Meadows BA

Writing for me is both creative and healing. Through the ages writing has been used as a form of catharsis, the Greek word for purifying the emotions. When we write about a particular event or experience, thought or feeling we release the emotion. We may wish to examine it or not, but in the act of transferring our thoughts onto paper, we have taken a large step towards self-healing. We should write it down: write it down and let it go.

Even before words were written down, bards, vocal poets and minstrels roamed the land from community to community, entertaining, enlightening, soothing and healing with their handed down tales and verse. People gathered round the communal fires to listen and to remember, enthralled at the magical power of the spoken word and some of these stories still survive in folk tale and legend. Tales of great loves and great wars now written down to help us understand that times may change but humans still suffer from the same emotional and physical symptoms as they have always done.

Suffering emotionally is a part of the human condition. Recently I read an article in the Holistic Health Magazine by the poet David Hart who was poet in residence for South Birmingham Mental NHS Trust. For a year he ran occupational therapy poetry sessions. He was in there, on the front line, teaching acutely mentally ill people how they can heal themselves though poetry as self expression; expression of feelings and it didn't matter to him whether these sick people were natural poets or not. They were thinking and feeling people. John Lennon once said that we are all poets because we all think, of course some of us feel more sensitively than others but we all feel too.

When I was awarded my honours degree from Salford University as a mature student in 1995, the elation that I felt was enormous. I had always nursed the ambition to become a teacher of English Literature and Language at secondary level and I thought I was well on my way. When I was offered a place at Edge Hill College the following year I was walking on air, big style. Then came the crash and I fell back down to earth with a thud when my eight year old son was diagnosed with cancer. Scott had a one in four million chance of developing the brain tumour which almost killed him.   Understandably, I was completely and utterly distraught, I lost over a stone in weight and other unpleasant physical, and emotional symptoms visited me, weakening my whole system. I lost the ability to write down what I was going through. I felt as though I had lost my vision, my voice. I desperately needed to be healed.   I thought that I would never again take pen to paper and feel the flow of creative thought soothing and easing my inner self. But I was wrong.

During Scott's recovery I was introduced to a wonderful healer, teacher and writer Marjorie Sutton BA founder of the Association of Professional Healers.   At first Marjorie began to heal my much depleted energy system. Through the counselling sessions, which form part of the healing process, it occurred to me that now Scott was on his way to full recovery, some of my anxiety came from the fact that I was not using my abilities and talents.   I had buried them, and even though Scott had come through, I felt that I was in some way a failure. Not only was I not a teacher but I was no longer a writer.   Marjorie asked me to write for the APH magazine.   I was hesitant inside but I heard myself saying yes. I now edit the magazine and have renamed it The APH Voice.

And because I am healed, I am now part of a scheme, backed by Preston Primary Care to promote awareness of mental health in the community.   I am teaching the therapeutic benefits of releasing those emotions into words.   Writing can be very relaxing, I know that.   In a safe environment where people understand that fears, doubts and pain can be let out and examined and let go of just like autumn leaves blowing away in the wind, thoughts and feelings cascade around, disperse and disappear. There is nothing more healing for the disquieted soul than the act of putting pen to paper, by writing.

SEIZE THE DAY

Conquering Writer's Block
with Vera Waters

When asked to run a workshop as part of the festival I decided that one of the biggest problems with which writers are beset is 'Writers Block' It is really about the positive and negative parts of the writers personality. We met together as a small group and proved without a doubt that 'good things often come in small packages.' How varied we all were, linked together by a common denominator....we all wanted to write !

As people from different walks of life, the members of the group set about the various tasks with interest and enthusiasm. We all had something to learn from each other and that included me. Once again I was reminded how unique people are, everyone with their own gifts and talents. An enjoyable morning with positive feedback, warmth and friendliness laced with deep and varied discussion. I hope that the participants enjoyed the experience and as a consequence felt more able to cope with that old, familiar adversary 'writers block'. Thank you for inviting me to run the workshop.

Vera Waters

Vera Waters is a life coach and counsellor. Her first book, Half A Rainbow – Insight into Stress, was published in 1990, and reprinted in 1996 Her second book, The Other Half of the Rainbow, went on to the market later that year. She is presently working on her third book A Mist of Rainbows which will reach the book shelves in late 2003.

ADIOS AMIGO
By Ken Taylor

Bonded by banter
we spent our free hours exploring caves, crags,
and 'piss-wet' mountains.

Obsessed by the notion
of being explorers.
we were also happy
to lie in the sun
and talk for Britain.

It was on such a day,
you told me about the fibrous snow,
piled on window sills
drifting neat,
curved against a factory wall.
Leeds lads, up to nothing good,
chucking snowballs of asbestos dust; arriving home
powder white.

Years later, high up
in the snow clad Rockies,
you were reunited with your snowballing chum.
For years he had
pleaded with you
to make the trip,
just get on a plane and come.

And your elation
once back home,
pulling photographs from a pile,
bubbling out your tale.

33

I called round
at the end
of a warm July,
 with its lilac buddleia
and cabbage whites.
You were lying
on a lounger,
gaunt, jaundiced.
 and very weak;
your bright words
and lively eyes
now dulled.

By December,
in a small varnished
side ward
at St Gemma's,
I joked
about the mayhem
of a particular climbing trip.
Unable to speak,
you answered with an opiate smile.

You once said, without bitterness,
'There are no Gods.'
I said there might be,
but unable to comprehend
their sense or purpose,
choose to leave them to their own devices.
Here on earth.
I preferred our friendship.

Adios amigo

THE MONGOLIAN
By Ken Taylor

We needed to find shelter:
we were a long way from the village,
and our clothing was inadequate for
the sudden storm that ravaged the
Steppes carrying grit charged with
inhuman cold. It stung exposed skin
and peppered the eyes.

To survive we had to push forward.
But the animals lay down, and would
not move. Their instinct was to
wait; so we had to remain, our backs
to their warm bellies. Their bulk
acting as a windbreak.

And they were right. From amongst
the dust and chilling gale, a cold sun
could occasionally be seen.. and this
veil of anti-life eventually passed

We stood and wept with relief The
animals rose, trembling, shaking the
grit from themselves, and brayed
as if they had something to celebrate.

Ken Taylor enjoys writing poetry and rock climbing. His
dream is to retire to France and make a living as a potter.

REMEMBRANCE

Memorial Poetry
With Caroline Gilfillan

Caroline brought a selection of objects which she arranged on the table. We could choose one to write about, or choose an object we had brought ourselves. She showed us how to write a series of thoughts relating to that object, which took us to a position where we could write a poem. We drew a timeline to include our relatives, friends, school, work, places, feelings and objects associated with them. It was surprising how many memories came back using this method.

We were given copies of the poem 'Handbag' by Ruth Fainlight to illustrate character depiction by using an object. We did an exercise visualising a person as an animal, weather, vegetable, drink and a car.

Photographs were used to produce a piece of work, by first of all writing down everything associated with that photograph and then producing a poem. Caroline Gilfillan made us all work very hard and gave us some useful ideas.

Glenda Charlesworth

Caroline Gilfillan is a published poet and tutor for the writing MA courses at Lancaster University. Her most popular work is a collection of poems 'Drowned in Overspill' published by Crocus Books.

BALLROOM COMPETITION
by Glenda Charlesworth

Hours of practice, rolled back carpet,
Book of footprints over her shoulder.
Full circle skirt cut out on the floor,
Tight fitting bodice, ten net underskirts,
Sparkly high heels, French pleated hair.
New suit for him, haircut and Brylcreem
Leather soled shoes, polished, shining
A handsome couple, gracefully glide,
My Prince and Princess go to the Ball.

GRANMA
by Glenda Charlesworth

Waste not, want not,
Make do and mend.
Grandma was an expert,
Nothing thrown away.
Sheets, ends to middled,
Buttons all were saved.
Cuffs on the dusters,
Rag rugs on the floor.

DRAGON
by Glenda Charlesworth

Blue, blue sky.
Spirit soaring.
Catching an updraft.
Today I fly.

HAT PIN
by Glenda Charlesworth

Every time she
Left the house
She pushed in the hat
Pin. I watched amazed
Expecting blood. I thought
That it went right through
Her head.

PEACE
by Glenda Charlesworth

Place your palms together
Evoke the still, small voice.
Ask your God for strength.
Calm your racing thoughts.
Everyone has this choice.

Glenda Charlesworth is at that 'funny age' of being not young but not old enough to draw a pension. She has survived Rock and Roll, Women's Lib, Flower Power, the Computer Revolution, a 33 year marriage and two children.

SOMETHING PRECIOUS
by Hazel Ratcliffe

A penniless student holds in his hands a gift wrapped with
care,
Eager recipient slowly unwraps.
Nestling there only two inches high, a figure of two little
mice,
Mrs. Mouse in pristine apron proudly holds her child's hand,
He stands there, eager for a response
His only words, "Mother and Son."

MY DAD – THOMAS
by Joan Hayward

Talking often and yet often silent
Holding grandchildren and withholding judgement
Open and comfortable, ordinary and special
My Dad, Bec's granddad.
Always there until you left
Suddenly, sickness, now at rest.

REMEMBRANCE
by Joan Hayward

Taken away, yet going resolutely
Holding and enjoying life till the end
Only sharing cares with your true love
Many people overflowed that place
And you were there, even though you'd gone
Still, often you return in memories, remembered.

Joan Hayward is a mother, daughter, sister, friend and
ordinary person.

STILLBIRTH
by Jackie Hayes

Screams
Through silence
Everlasting waves of
Pain
Heat of neverending
August night. I
Never held you
I never even saw you. But you are
Ever in my heart.

EVACUEE
by Jackie Hayes

Mouse-like she came
into my life,
but grew sleeker and more confident,
cat-contented when
she married.
Dark noisy wartime nights
had brightened into fun.
Shy days of sharing pop and sherbet
now behind her,
she is lavish with hors d'oeuvres
and good red wine,
Vera Lynn love-songs of our
backyard concerts now
come true.

DEVALUED
by Jackie Hayes

She points her toe
arm raised
a tiny ballerina
fashioned in porcelain,
reminder of his little girl
back home.

Tucked close inside
his uniform breast pocket
she nestled safe –
until he bent to
shoulder kitbag
when her dainty skirt
of fine pierced china
snapped.

'How could you be so careless?'
mother scolded.
'See. its spoiled.'
Later, a knowledgeable friend
pronounced it quite devalued.
'Pity that, might have been
worth a bit.

But that's the way of war.
All's damaged.
Every value overthrown.

DAYS GONE BY
by Carla Bee

Back in '76, when I was 21
A proud nurse I was.

With the plain blue dress and the white
starched collars.
Scissors on a chain and old fob watches
Telling time in every way.

Strict on the ward from Matron
it was, beds to be made,
bed pans to be washed.

Finished my duties, a day
has been done.
Marching past Matron's Office
to the solace of the Nurse's Home.

Time to go to the doctor's parties,
Best Dressed in every way.
and drinking cheap red wine.

The doctors drank the beer
And the whiskey made them frisky.
Time to make my move
on doctor sneaky pants!

Carla Bee qualified as a nurse at age 21. Prior to a serious
riding accident, she was a very active sportswoman,
swimming and waterskiing.

TO MY DAD

by Ivy Carroll

On the occasion of the double wedding of friends' daughters

Do you remember that Autumn Day
The day the girls were wed.
Edna was bridesmaid
At St. Saviour's Church, instead
Of that Chapel – (not good enough) – it's true.
The Church had a red carpet, and the bells
And hymns – well one or two,
And yet the Church smelled musty
Damp showed on the red tiled floor.
The sweeter smells were of the flowers
And that buttonhole of yours.
Well that was after the panic
When you'd lost it back at home,
"It's by your suit" – "Oh no it's not"
It's in the cool, inside a clay pot."
"Now calm yourself down, you fool".
And when the folk came from the Church
To have their photos taken
Now with Mum and Dad, and then the lads
And Gran must not be forsaken!
I took this snap of you that day
You stood by Mum, Fran and James.
The resulting photo I made just of you
Cut out and now forever framed,
Cut off from friends – Mum was tickled pink,
All you could think of was "Where's my cigs
And a cup of tea to drink."
You enjoyed that day, the meal, the fun,
You did, I'm sure your share
You'd play some tricks – it wouldn't be you
Unless – but – by then I wasn't there!!

Ivy Carroll is now retired but co-ordinates the Wheelton & Withnell Care Cars and is also Secretary of Withnell & Dist. Pensioner's Assoc.

SOAP SUDS

Script Writing
with Helen Eatock

If you ever wondered how our favourite TV soaps are written you should have come to this workshop. Helen Eatock, who has written for Emmerdale and other TV soaps and theatre productions, took us through the story-lining procedure. Beginning with a brief and four characters, the group, aided by Helen, created additional characters and planned their dramatic lives; plotted their stories into episodes; and finally into co-coordinating scenes which not only avoided having characters in two places at once, but also provided cliff-hangers for end of episodes and commercial breaks. Her handouts on avoiding pitfalls and poor practice are very useful.

A practical workshop, it provided a real insight into script-writing, at the end of which most of us declared that we never knew script writing was so involved....

Carol Thistlethwaite

Helen Eatock is a professional script writer for television. She has written extensively for Crossroads, ITV1; Byker Grove, BBC1; Emmerdale, ITV1; Children's Ward, ITV1; Grange Hill, BBC1; Dream Team, Sky1. Helen is also a scriptwriting tutor at the University of Salford.

ALL'S FAIR

by Evelyn Crompton

I. EXT. AT THE CREMATORIUM

MAGGIE has come to brother's funeral. By her side is her daughter CHLOE. Heads are turning to stare at them.

>   CHLOE
> They're all staring at you, Mum.

>   MAGGIE
> I wasn't invited, and everyone is wondering who you are.

>   CHLOE
> They all look as if they are dressed for a wedding. *We* are dressed for a funeral.

>   **CUT TO**

2. EXT. FAIRGROUND

Fairground music. Stalls with people looking and buying.

>   STALL HOLDERS
> Come and try your luck!

A child pestering its mum

>   CHILD
> I want an ice cream!

>   **CUT TO**

3. <u>EXT. GROUNDS of the CREMATORIUM</u>

Mourners have moved away from the grave and are standing in groups, except for MAGGIE and CHLOE who are on their own. They are about to walk away when DANNY comes up to them.

> DANNY
> What are *you* doing here Maggie?

> MAGGIE
> I have the right. Archie was my brother. This is my daughter Chloe.

> DANNY
> Thee ought to have visited a long time ago. How long has it been?

> MAGGIE
> I haven't been counting but it has been a long time. I have had my reasons for not coming. I want to pay my last respects. Is the business doing well?

> DANNY
> Since my Dad passed away, I have been in charge; a role that he would have approved of. Come along, now that you are here, have some lunch with us. It's all prepared in the caravan that I use.

A female mourner has burst into tears.

>   MAGGIE
> It's Anoushka! She thought a lot of
> Archie.

>   DANNY
> You could say that. She can turn the
> tap on, and she can't tell fortunes in
> that state. And seeing that she's our
> only fortune teller ...

**ANOUSHKA comes over. DANNY walks
away.**

>   ANOUSHKA
> Maggie, it's lovely to see you. I'm so
> glad you came. I do miss Archie.
> (Dabs her eyes) And he was so
> popular, I don't think that Danny will
> be able to compete but he will soon
> own the business. The Will is being
> read after lunch. I'm sorry, who is
> this lovely young lady?

>   MAGGIE
> (Smiling for the first time)
>   My daughter Chloe.
>   (looking serious)
> I did miss Archie when I left the
> fairground. I missed all of you. My
> relationships didn't work out.

> ANOUSHKA
> Don't blame yourself.
> You've been unlucky.

As they start to walk towards the funeral cars they can hear children laughing

> ANOUSHKA
> I love to hear children laughing. I wish I'd been blessed.

> MAGGIE
> You're still young enough to have children. You may be lucky one day.

> ANOUSHKA
> Near the fairground there's a Children's Home, so I'm reminded every day.

CUT TO

4. **INT. CHILDRENS HOME**

A BOY about ten yrs is changing out of his school uniform and hiding it. He looks furtively around before leaving.

CUT TO

5.INT. INSIDE DANNY'S CARAVAN
Fairground music can be heard.

DANNY
I hope you've all enjoyed the meal?

ALL
Yes,yes, very nice. Thank you.

DANNY
Good. It's what Dad would have wanted. The music is rather loud for this occasion. I think we can dispense with it, until the Will has been read. (Smiles) The solicitor will be here shortly. I won't be long.

CUT TO

6. EXT. THE FAIRGROUND
DANNY walks to the Candy Floss car.

DANNY
Hello Jack, Eli. I'm going to switch the music off. When the solicitor has left, turn it on again. (Looks round) There's a boy near the roundabout machinery. I've seen him here before.

DANNY goes over to the BOY who sneaked out of the children's home.

49

DANNY
What do you think you're doing?

BOY
I ain't doing anything wrong. What's it
got to do with you, anyway?

DANNY
I happen to own this fairground.

BOY
My name's Ben. Can I work for you
one day?

DANNY
You've got some growing-up to do.
When that day arrives, come and see
me.

CUT TO

7. EXT. CANDY FLOSS CAR

DANNY
You know when to put the music
 back on, Jack. I've had a word with
the boy.

JACK
He's scarpered now. The solicitor's
arrived. I've seen him before, when
your father was alive, God rest his
soul.

50

JACK watches DANNY walk away.
He speaks to his wife ELI

> JACK
> Eli, I've never seen him look as
> happy. I would be, too, in his shoes.
> (He slaps her bottom)

> ELI
> Not in front of the customers, Jack.

> JACK
> We haven't got any yet. There's only
> the goat tethered over there. It's been
> ~~bleeding~~ *bleating* since the early
> hours.

> ELI
> So would you be, tethered there since
> last night.

CUT TO

8. INT. CARAVAN
The SOLICITOR is seated behind a table.
**He is looking at Archie's family sitting in front
of him.**

> SOLICITOR
> I can see that you have dressed
> appropriately, as Archie requested, all
> in bright colours.

51

MAGGIE and CHLOE glance at one another.

> SOLICITOR
> When Archie was alive, he instructed
> me to thank everyone on his behalf
> for their loyalty and for working hard
> to make the business a success.
> First, I have to mention an employee.
> To Jack, Archie has Bequeathed the
> goat.
> > (Coughs)
> Archie left his son, Danny, his
> caravan and his motorbike. To
> Maggie, his only sister, he has
> bequeathed the business.

Gasps from everybody.
DANNY'S smile disappears, and he walks out.

To be continued..........

Evelyn Crompton is the secretary of Ashton Writer's
Literary Club. She is a compulsive writer and has
published a children's story called Hedgerow Hill. She
is now in the throes of pruning an adult novel.

BURN IT

Song Writing for Teenagers
With Geoff Dixon

'Sign of the Times' has always been an inspiring place for me to work with its hi-tech equipment, vivid décor and most of all the young people that bring it to life. The All Write Festival was no exception. The creative song making day was a great success and although we didn't have the number of participants we were expecting we certainly got quality of writing.

The day started with an introduction to songwriting, looking at song structures, lyrics and melodies and seeing how hit songs have been constructed. Then the young people set about writing their own hit song with the help of myself and a little bit of the SOTT inspiration.........We then transferred the masterpieces into recorded form using the SOTT studio. The writers even had the bravery to face a performance and sung their own tracks. This was their very first venture into a recording studio.

The results, although we ran out of time, were fantastic and hopefully will prove to be a lasting record of a great day in Eccleston.

Geoff Dixon

Geoff Dixon specialises in music workshops for community projects and youth groups. He is based at MMORMUSIC in Morecambe

WHEN I MET TILLY.
by Jack Donnelly

When I met Tilly I was quivering.
She was two years younger than me.
But that didn't really bother me.
We looked! And winked! And smiled.

She had long brown hair.
With a lovely wide smile.
She's so beautiful.
With big blue eyes.

The next day came, she looked fabulous.
Her hair was hanging right down.
We got so close as close as friends.
And sometimes we'd go out.

And I just couldn't stop thinking about her.
And I just couldn't stop looking straight at her.

She had long brown hair.
With a lovely wide smile.
She's so beautiful.
With big blue eyes.

I wish she could know how I feel.
If only she knew how I feel — today.

She had long brown hair.
With a lovely wide smile.
She's so beautiful.
With big blue eyes.

54

STORY OF KATIE
by Adam Frackelton

It was a sunny day, 100 degrees.
I was outside washing the car.
When I noticed a girl, who was new on the street
Carrying an electric guitar.

We eventually met, down at Birchwood park,
Tried to hide my sweaty palms.
But with her long blonde hair and sweet perfume
I couldn't resist her charms.

I felt myself falling in to her arms.

This is not a love song, this Is not a good song.
This is just a simple rhyme.
About a girl. About a boy.
About a moment in time.

So time went by, as fast as it does,
Good friends turned into lovers.
The living was great, sexy and cool,
And we loved our way through four summers.

Eventually drifted apart, we weren't getting on
For weeks and weeks I missed her.
But the pain and the tears came to an end
As soon as I met Melissa.

I felt myself falling to kiss her.

This is not a love song, this Is not a good song.
This is just a simple rhyme.
About a girl. About a boy.
About a moment in time.

This is not a love song, this is not a good song.
This is just a simple rhyme.
About a girl. About a boy.
About a moment in time.

BEGINNINGS AND ENDINGS

A reading workshop
with Anne Caldwell

This workshop attracted a lot of participants, all keen to promote reading. Anne Caldwell gave us handouts of beginnings and endings of certain novels which we discussed. We were asked to recommend a book we had recently read and enjoyed and then explain why we enjoyed it. We also talked about our reading habits and some of our favourite titles, which varied considerably.

All the participants were keen to start a reading group and a date was set to meet up again. One participant kindly offered a free venue for future meetings. At our second meeting enough people attended to start two reading groups. This was most gratifying as when we attempted to set up a group last year only two people turned up.

Gwen Weiss

Anne Caldwell is not only a Literature Development worker but also a published poet featured in the Virago Collection of Women's Poetry. Her work is currently displayed in the NW Libraries poster campaign for National Poetry Day 2003.

FOR MY SON, ANTON

by Anne Caldwell

I am learning to live in the moment,

Watching you strut from lounge to
Kitchen, proud as a king in my fake fur hat.

You inspect each floorboard for lost beads,
Peer out of the cat flap at a world

Beyond five stone steps – an Inca temple,
A jungle of cracked concrete and dandelion clocks.

Yesterday, three kitchen drawers were full
Of forbidden treasure. I shrieked as you fell silent,

Wandered casually back into the room
with a chisel and two 60watt light bulbs.

The theory of iridology argues that
Every iris-fleck can signal a chapter of a life:

Mine are steely grey with
Too much watching and waiting in the corridors

Of other people's lives.
Yours are clear – blue as a jay's wing.

You are centre stage as you take a few first steps
Across your very own red carpet.

CHILD'S PLAY

Writing for Children
With Jane Eagland

This was a very enjoyable workshop, packed with tips and information. The leader started by distributing copies of lots of children's books for everyone to look at. Then she had a series of exercises the first of which was a character profile of someone we wished to write about (real or imagined).

Next we looked at story openings, ways of depicting characters and deciding whose point of view the story should be told from. Later we were given advice on the different requirements for children of different ages, and where to look for ideas. We also did mind-mapping. We were given help on understanding the market and information about what publishers want and also what they don't want.

Finally we were asked to 'grab a reader' using the person we had profiled at the beginning of the workshop, establish setting, problem or what the person wanted to achieve in 250 words. This was a very useful and informative workshop for anyone wanting to try their hand at children's writing. One lady had to leave at lunchtime and she was sorry to have to do so.

Gwen Weiss

After teaching English for 26 years, **Jane Eagland** gained an M.A.in creative writing at Lancaster University. She has been successful in poetry and short story competitions and the Andersen press is to publish her first picture book story for children.

SECRET NUMBER
by Louise Krafchick

Myrtle slid back the mud spattered sleeve of her T shirt to reveal the secret number inked on the inside of her skinny forearm.

Fear travelled up the length of her legs and met the fear that had journeyed from the pit of her stomach. They now converged and thundered inside her chest.

She slid the card into the thin metal mouth. It asked for the secret number which she'd heard her mother rhyme off......

HERO
By John A Stewart

"No!" shouted Ben. The focus of Toni's glare shifted slowly from his grip on Amy's crisp packet around to Ben's fearful eyes.

Through his gritted teeth Tom hissed, "What has this got to do with you?"

Ben's skinny body could not decide whether to attempt a menacing posture or, wither into the disguise of an autumn leaf and drift quietly away down to the other end of the school yard on a chilly breeze.

What Ben did know was what was right. Nobody should steal crisp packets, especially not one that belonged to his best friend Amy.

PONY RIDE
By Marcia Ashford

Becca landed on the grass with a thud, still hanging on to the halter rope. Vanessa her pony jumped sideways again – very nervy.

The usually quiet shallow river had risen to a rushing torrent. How to get home?

Her Mum had dropped her off by the road at the gate. Usually they forded the stream and went home in ten minutes. If she went by road she would be late for the gymkhana.

Becca and Vanessa moved nervously along the bank looking for a shallower part. They came to the bend in the river and a weir. Becca realised she could use the top of the weir as stepping-stones......

BULLIED
by A. Valenzia

The best hidden way to school was through some back gardens, behind the hedges and down the little lane by the side of the park. But to get there David still had to cross two more streets.

David peeped round the corner. Was it clear?

His heart sank. He could see them waiting, leaning against a wall, there were four of them today.

What next?

He might try to creep away, find another longer way to school.

He might then be spotted.

He might try and run the gauntlet.

A bigger fiend might appear and offer to help him take them on.

He might try to outrun them

FRIENDSHIP
by Gwen Weiss

"Argh!" Lindsey jumped to her feet.

"What's up?" asked Jo, still sitting on the grass, dangling her feet in the cool water of the stream.

"Look, there's an enormous beetle."

Jo now leapt to her feet as well and the pair stood paralysed as the shiny black creature disappeared behind a small rock.

"I'm terrified of beetles. One nipped me last year," Lindsey said, her eyes round with fear.

"I was stung with a bee, on my foot. It really hurt and I cried. Becky Simpson was there. She just laughed and called me a cry-baby. Then everyone joined in. I hate her!"

"Oh she's a real dork. No-one really likes her but she's always got lots of sweets so…!"

"She's a cheat too. She got real nasty when I wouldn't let her copy my homework."

They had quite forgotten the beetle by this time.

"My mum says she's like that because deep down she's unhappy. Do you think if we try to be friends she might be nicer to us?"

"No way!" said Lindsey, tossing her long red curls. "You can do what you want but just don't try to make *me* be friends with *her.*"

Later as Jo was walking home she met Becky who for once was minus a couple of her cronies. Tentatively Jo smiled and to her surprise Becky smiled back.

" Do you want a toffee?" she asked.

Lindsay hesitated then shook her head. "No thanks, I'm just off home for my tea," adding to her own amazement, "do you want to come too?"

BIFFY
by E. Valenzia

Biffy was an odd kind of bird, even for a duck. To begin with, he didn't look like other ducks. He was white, but had a longer neck than most ducks but his head was fortunately or unfortunately very duck like.

It was fortunate because it meant he at least looked like he belonged with other water fowl in Patchden Park and unfortunate because it meant that Biffy stuck out. His Mother called him Biffy because his brothers and sisters used to go – BIFF IT and butt him when they were all swimming along behind her.

"Thanks," said the little duckling to his Mother, "Now they'll hit me even more."

"It's his fault," said Tupper who was the oldest of all the ducklings. "He biffs us and then we all go BANG into each other."

So the poor duckling began to swim behind his brothers and sisters. This meant that Biffy stuck out like the ugly duckling in the tale. This drew attention of people passing by, people who came just to admire and feed the ducks.

But not everyone wanted to feed the ducks, one small boy threw stones at them........

IN THE PICTURE

Poetry and Art
With Alison Chisholm

Are you one of those people who find themselves wondering how to fill a formidable blank sheet of paper with poetry? Well Alison Chisholm had the answers. Lucky to have a free range of Astley Hall, writers were found sitting on stairways, in cosy nooks, quiet courtyards and on the hard exhibition floor scribbling poems. She provided us with lots of ideas about how to create poems from very different pictures and art work. The exercises were well structured and by the end of the day even the newest writer was able to complete the challenge of writing a poem from a surreal print in less than 10 minutes. Alison's useful handouts also mean we should never be stuck for writing ideas again.

Carol Thistlethwaite

Alison Chisholm teaches creative writing, and is the author of seven poetry collections, and books, articles and a correspondence course on the craft of writing poetry. Her most recent work will appear in 'Mapping the Maze,' to be published by Headland in the near future.

64

MONA LISA

by Elizabeth Parish

I'd like to slap her silly face –
She looks so smug.
Hands folded on her lap,
She's staring back at me
so knowingly.

Sure of herself
as I am not.
She sits and waits
as if she knows
what is to come – except
she doesn't realise
I'd like to slap her face.

ESCHER MOONSCAPE

by Elizabeth Parish

Without the framing walls
loud-speaking moons
shout at the tesselated room.

Aeolian horns hang soundless
in windless windows.

Human-headed harpies in and out
echo the room, but do not hear
the speaking moon.

A STUDY IN AMBIGUITY

(Portrait of Elizabeth Tudor)
by Elizabeth Parish

Roses stud her frame
and decorate her person,
Yet she wears
large pearl drops in her ears
and around her throat,
while the crescent moon
balanced against her breasts
echoes the shadows
underneath her heavy-lidded eyes.

Her crown rests lightly
almost carelessly; the sceptre too
seems idle in her hand.
And yet she holds the orb protectively
nestled in her arm
beneath the regal ermine robe
as it to keep her world secure.

PORTRAITS AT ASTLEY HALL
by Elizabeth Parish

Be impressed.
In gilded frames
we stand about the entrance hall
like footmen –
though our attitudes do not suggest
we're here to wait on you.

We wait for you
to notice us.
Remark our names and titles
and reflect
on all our many genealogies.

Ignore the paintings hung above us,
the escutcheons. And forget
anachronistic additions
such as notices and cameras.
We are of the fabric of the place,
We belong.

We matter.
We are of the age
of Astley:

explorers of the world,
Magellan, Drake,
and of the mind,
Mahomet and Spinoza.
Rulers of the world,
Alva and Farnese, Tamburlain
of France and Sweden.

Notice how Robert Dudley

turns his back on Queen Elizabeth
and she on him.

Between them mottos,
Fabula divisit amicos
and *Rumor acerbe tace* –
even in this place
there's back-stairs gossip.

We can never mount the stairs
nor walk about the house,
but only stare our dignity.

Before you leave
look, do not stare at us,
but be impressed.

AT HOME
by Elizabeth Parish

There are too many things I want to do
or things I have to do
to put away the residue
before I start on something new.

I might grow bored
and want to pick it up again.

Quick - someone's at the door!
Let's just shove everything
under the chaise-longue out of sight....

Too late.
Please do come in,
sit down... oh!
Just a minute while I clear a space.

COLOUR ME.....
by Elizabeth Parish

I got the jacket-habit from my blazer.
I loved my blazer, bought for school
from Foster's, Ealing Broadway.
No one else I knew wore anything
so challenging and so sophisticated.
All the other pieces of the uniform
seemed drabber in comparison
and ordinary beside my blazing blazer.

So I peacocked around, imagining myself
The cynosure of eyes: among my peers
the odd one out, but safe in school
among the uniform kingfisher greens.

The jackets in my wardrobe now
are cinnamon and navy, singing lilac.
Best of all, the one in palest jade,
Faint echo of my childhood pride.

Elizabeth Parish has been working with words for more years than she cares to remember. Since retirement, she has become a member of the Salford Women Writers group, and devotes much time to writing - particularly poetry.

SILK ON CANVAS
by Ruth Goode

Three dimensional patterns
produce kites flying troubled skies.
Silky lilac hues soothe
while slime-green circles
form mysterious ponds.
Rust brown spheres loom
like global omens,
raven black squiggles
are deep seated misery.

ABSTRACT
by Ruth Goode

I am a black dot
inside a red swirl
enclosed in a purple square.
Critics call me a Representation
but I am trapped
stunted by the artist
a full stop.

HOPE
by Ruth Goode

(inspired by Mlilais painting "The Blind Girl")

A tattered blind lady,
clasps the hand of her child.
Prays against oncoming storms.
Crows raucous omens,
trees staunch against wintry winds.
Rainbows hint at happiness.
A butterfly
dance-teases hope.
Squeeze-box songs sing
to keep them both alive,
when she sings by the wayside
desiring a different life,
one where her eyes would open
and see her precious child.

Ruth Goode is an avid reader; she also plays the piano, is re-learning French and loves animals. Ruth has had a number of poems published in various anthologies and Never Bury Poetry magazine.

PORTRAIT OF A YOUNG WOMAN
by Carol Thistlethwaite

Who are you, looking over your shoulder
from centuries away?

Your hand lifts your skirt ready to walk,
and a silky shawl wisps low from shoulders,
slipping,
as if it would fall
to the ground
revealing some truth,
or whispering fantasies that swirl
beneath controlled satin hair,
held in taut ringlets,
and bound in bunches over each ear?

As guarded allure
escapes the frame,
I wonder…

is the space you walk into your own time and place,
or do you take me to my own hiding place?

VANITY

by Carol Thistlethwaite

Will you dance with me and my serpent
charm?
Will you love me as I love myself?
I am vain, I am selfish, I will lure you away
To the place I embrace myself.
With my arms round my waist,
And my hands hugging hips,
Part of me is still fading away,
My home is a skull
Where there is little goodwill
for anyone
- except myself.

I am sad, I am lonely,
I will walk empty planks
That stretch out to a bare beyond.
I will take you and waste you
And drain you alive,
Then prey on somebody else.

Carol Thistlethwaite is a graduate from Edge Hill
university college where she is about to begin an MA in
writing studies. Carol is a new writer who explores many
forms including visual poetry; she is published in several
anthologies, journals and magazines.

TIME
by Joan Hayward

Written in response to a Dali painting

Grains of sand make desert
Grains of dust make man
From dust to dust life passes
Hold it whilst you can

Eternity both comes and goes
Yet all of life stands still
Life's storms and joys pass ever onward
Unaltered by man's will

GOING FOR GURNARD
by Chris Collison

Inspired by Escher's Whirlpools

Around the red gurnard the grey gurnard gyrated.
Did the grey gurnard gyrate graciously around the red
gurnard?
The grey gurnard gyrated grumpily around the red gurnard.
Gloriously gyrating gurnard generates great joy.
Grumpily gyrating gurnard goes into great grub.
Good eating if not gladly gyrating
-- grudgingly good.

74

CHAOS

By Glenda Charlesworth

If I had   a tidy room?
Would I have   a tidy mind?
If I had   a tidy mind?
   Would I still be a poet?

WIND

By Glenda Charlesworth

Has this wind that ruffles my hair,
flares my skirt, come far?
Has it whipped the ocean crests
or traced wave lines in the desert?
Where will it go from here?
Will it cross another ocean
and in the tropical heat
meet other winds
to create a tornado?

PEARLS
by Alison Chisholm

Freed from their thread,
a waterfall of miniature moons
spills over my hand,
fills each dark crevice in the drawer,
no outfall, these,
from dragons fighting in the sky,
nor some oblation poured for Isis,
but most precious of my wedding gifts.

Now, even scattered in the dull of wood,
each crystal's axis catches light,
reflects, refracts soft rainbows. I collect
a handful, scoop them up,
pick through chains and scarves and boxes
to secure each globe.

Only when the string is drawn once more,
when eye and hand have fixed their graduation,
do I find the grasp of pearls is tighter,
and some beads must have eluded searching fingers.
Solitary as in their oyster womb
they glimmer in corners, nacred with dust.

But errant pearls do not diminish
they enhance the necklace,
clutch its promises,
concentrate its lustre.

I know again the first feel
of smooth rounds circling my neck,
glow of their creamy orient,
cool clasp of angels' tears a talisman
for luck and love.

THE OAK ROOM
Astley Hall
by Vivienne M. Artt.

I step
from morning sun
to the sombre darkness
and sobriety of the hail.

I pass with deference
the portraits of imposing men —
censorious, proprietal,
darkly grim.

As I climb, stairs creak
and floors complain
like old men under olive trees
resting in the sun....

In the Oak Room
stone-mullioned sunlight
floods the space,
the room's awash —
wood panelling gleams,
four-poster bed is jet,
in the hooded, amber cradle
a baby deeply dreams.

77

Somewhere out of sight
a woman sings
and for an instant
I am she —
invisible but blessed,
richly robed in happiness,
mother of a bygone age,
mistress of a gilded cage....

The singing stops.
I tip-toe to the window —
across the blue hydrangeas
lie shady waters
where ducks dabble
and lilies spread their pads.

Within the room
the iridescent silence waits
while I retreat across the floor,
the tapestries hang mutely, and
the lace-enfolded infant sleeps
exactly as before.

Vivienne Artt is a native of Ulster but has spent the last 26
yrs in the Red Rose County which she has grown to love.
She is passionate about poetry and values it as a source of
understanding, wisdom and vision. Her other interests
include art, Music, History and Travel.

LAUS VENERIS -- IN PRAISE OF VENUS
by Mike Cracknell
from the painting by Sir Edward Burne-Jones

Three long years fighting the Saracens,
Five white knights crusading for the cause,
All that time without a woman,
They have come back from the wars,
Ardently in search of whores.

When they arrive at the local brothel,
Five scarlet women are waiting inside.
All of them have lost their chastity,
Most of them have lost their pride,
Paid to keep men satisfied.

The madam sits at the head of the table.
A golden crown rests on her knee.
She is about to make some money,
Her girls will not perform for free.
They are ladies of pedigree.

On the floor lies a fallen rose,
A memory of one with whom she'd lain.
A prince who also went to battle.
A lover who was savagely slain.
Her heart still bears the pain.

Now the knights leap from their chargers
Eager to mount the ladies instead,
Lances all prepared for action,
Each passionate as if newly-wed.
At long last some action in bed.

ON SEEING A PORTRAIT OF CROMWELL
by Mike Cracknell

You stand with sober authority, surrounded by sombre shadows.
You have prevailed in the holy struggle to seize paramount power,
the power to puritanise the nation and depose
the despotic, papist monarch.
You are the victorious general of Marston Moor and Naseby,
the curse of the cavaliers, the bringer of austerity,
self styled Lord Protector.
The fading light picks out the shining armour on the strong right arm
used to sign the King's death warrant.
You know that God is on your side.

Your face is sanitized by the lack of natural defects.
Even the highest moral principles can succumb
to personal vanity.
On another occasion you demanded "Warts and all"
but not this time.
The white collar is tinged with dingy grey.
Do your eyes betray the ruthlessness of a bigoted tyrant?
Is there a flicker of doubt, a hint of ultimate failure?
Is absolute power in the early stages of absolute corruption?

FIRST FISH
by Mike Cracknell

As I sat by the water I struggled to focus
my wandering mind on the tiny white float.
For eons it remained monotonously motionless,
unless disturbed by the wash of a boat.

Below the float was a weighted line and
a hook with two maggots dangling.
I was minding my dad's rod until his return
even though I was scornful of angling.

Sweltering and bored, I daydreamed a bit,
languidly scanning the somnolent scene.
Everything, everywhere seemed at first sight
To be in some subtle shade of green.

Nature had studied a paint colour chart.
She had tried different hues, here and there.
I imagined names for each nuance of tint
as I lethargically slouched in the chair.

The mirror like surface of the canal was olive;
there were mallard, lily pad, willow and reed.
I saw spruce and meadow grass beyond the far bank.
I didn't notice a fish start to feed.

Caterpillar, holly, cheese and onion crisp packet
were just some of the tones I could see.
Then suddenly, in a panic, I realized
that the greenest all was me.

That unwatched float had now disappeared.
I heaved the rod up towards the sky.
The green and red perch was well and truly hooked,
and from that moment on so was I.

81

MY SIDE
by Mike Cracknell

There are two sides to every argument,
two sides to every bed.
My side is complemented by the presence of
pens, paper,
notebooks, newspapers,
reference books, magazines
thesaurus, dictionary,
poet's manual, rhyming dictionary,
works of favourite poets, anthologies,
Alison Chisholm's Practical Poetry Course,
Competitions Bulletin, Small Press Guide.
A comprehensive collection of poetic paraphernalia,
a veritable cornucopia of knowledge
overflowing with literary scholarship or
"that untidy heap of rubbish"
as the voice from the
women's magazine, make-up,
perfume bottle, earring,
coffee cup, handbag
side of the bed would say.

Mike Cracknell is a member of Writers Inc. and Preston
Poets' Society. He worked for forty years in the rubber
industry as a polymer chemist before retiring earlier this
year to devote more time to writing. To date he seems to
have found even less time to write. Interests include
performing poetry, running quizzes, rabbits, all kinds of
music and all kinds of sport, in particular Preston North
End.

OF HER FRIEND
by Ken Taylor

She said
he was a mild looking man,
that
leukaemia and watercolours
were his last
two years.

She never,
understood his death,
nothing was finished,
but his life,
which he required.

Against a grey
drizzled sky
and galvanized netting,
sweetpeas sit
pulsating their wings.
May they long choose
to alight here,
where his colour was always
welcome.

BLUE VAPOUR - A PAINTING
by Ken Taylor

Cooling towers in a large landscape,
discharge blue vapour
into a fresh, constant wind.

There are kids in the distance, larking about,
deep into a game of tumbles and laughter.
Directly above,
paragliders put their lives on hold
and hover. One is so close
you can hear the flap of sail cloth.

Down across the valley
the blue vapour moves on,
delicately dissipating
into this illusion.

WHAT'S SO FUNNY???

Stand up comedy with Janice Connolly and Archie Kelly

A workshop with a difference because it was performance orientated and spread over two days. A number of the participants had expected to simply write comedy routines, not perform them as well. This led to the first joke – 'I'm in the wrong workshop' and one or two people incorporated it into their routines. Both workshop leaders were experienced professional stand up comedians as well as being actors and singers and well informed about comedy genres. We discussed different comedians, and analysed their styles of material and delivery; explored different types of comedy from slapstick to satire; watched Archie Kelly deliver his routine and then tentatively tried out a short routine of our own.

Having built up some confidence, the group concentrated on writing material using methods such as juxtaposition, one liners, puns and topicality. Having developed material the group progressed to performance, and learnt microphone techniques, how to open and close the routine, what to do if nobody laughs and how to put down hecklers. Moving from the security of a closed workshop to performing on the open stage was something of a shock. However all the performers managed their acts without serious trauma and one even got a booking.

Margot Agnew

Janice Connolly and **Archie Kelly** are cast members of the comedy series Phoenix Nights shown on Channel 4. Janice has an alter ego as Mrs Barbara Nice. Both comedians can be seen performing in comedy venues in the North West.

DEFROCKED
by Jim Salt

The village niggardly nuisance and troublesome transvestite George Eena was again arrested. This time his victim was Spice Rice, one of the touring singers of the Chinese pop group The Rice Girls. George accused Spice Rice of stealing his best dress.

It all began when George arrived home drunk and discovered his entire collection of dresses stolen. On leaving the house to report the theft to the Police he thought he saw Spice Rice wearing his favourite dress. He began to threaten her and was told to calm down by local preacher and idealist Hugh Topia. George reacted by battering Hugh with his own Bible. The village book shop owner Ann Thology ran to rescue Hugh and George battered her too. She later said, 'After this episode he deserves a long sentence. Full stop!'

Spice Rice fled but George caught her outside the wallpaper shop and gave her an awful pasting. Counter assistants Polly Filla and Matt Finish ran out to help Spice Rice and were also attacked. Spice Rice ran across the road and hell for leather through the shoe shop. Sole proprietor Jack Boot and assistant manager Cherie Blossom grabbed George but he struggled free.

Passing restaurant owner Chris P Noodles and friend of Spice Rice made a citizen's arrest. With help from health club owner Jim Nasium, George was frogmarched to the Police Station. On arrival desk sergeant Mickey Taker said to George, 'No more dressing up for you for a while. You're due for a dressing down.' George turned violent again when Jim Nasium added 'Yes George this time it could be Holloway for you'. Suddenly in walked George's lawyer Lou Pole who began harassing Mickey and Jim for harassing George.

George and Lou were then booked for disturbing the peace. Two minutes later came an unexpected development in the form of Henry Etta, another transvestite. He said he had come to confess to the stealing of George's dresses and stated that his accomplice was Lou Pole. Lou attacked Henry, and called him a traitor. George attacked Lou and Henry and called them both traitors. Mickey Taker, Jim Nasium and Chris P. Noodles joined in the scuffle and eventually the three transvestites were behind bars.

Since then the developers have gone to town on the village and soon the village will be a town. However, before this happens the village may qualify for a place in the Guinness Book of Records as the only village on the verge of becoming a town that is holding in the Police Station a trio of very cross cross dressers.

Jim Salt is a member of the Ex Files. Ex building site worker, ex - self employed turf layer and gardener and then ex school caretaker. He is also a member of the RSPB and interested in all things natural and sometimes things unnatural.

ANYBODY FOR A DATE
by Joan Patrick

I was in the charity shop looking for bargains when I bumped into my friend Beverley. I hadn't seen her for ages, I hardly recognised her, she'd got a ring in her nose and her hair spiked up.

She said she'd left her ex; the kids were in care and she'd joined one of those speed dating agencies. She said you get five minutes with each chap then a bell rings and it's all change. There's usually about twenty four men there.

She said if you find one you like you can arrange another meeting, or take him home. Beverley thought she would take him home but they flatly refused to let him in at the Home for Battered Wives, so he asked her to go to his place. I asked her what he was like, she said he wasn't very tall, has his own home, but only has a little Rover.

He has a tatty tom cat which he took in when the folks next door kicked it out because of it's bad habits. He felt sorry for it so he bought it a big bag of cat litter but it didn't like it so it has to have Choosy.

She said his name's Horace Occlestone - she meant the chap not the cat. I said fancy calling a little baby Horace with a name like Occlestone.

I asked her what he was like upstairs, meaning was he brainy? She said she didn't know about upstairs being that he lived in a bungalow. I said it was his intellect I was asking about.

She told me she'd met a few others at these speed dating agencies but she couldn't make her mind up. I asked her to call at our house and we'd make a list of the positives and negatives, but I had to hurry home for the gas man.

She came that night, I was just cleaning up after the parrot, oh they do make a mess. Anyway this is how it went.

No 1. Horace Occlestone

No 2. Tom; rented house, had no door on his toilet, was obsessed with fast cars. She said when he took her on a trip to Wales he got up to ninety miles an hour on the M 56. She asked him what would happen if he had to brake. He told her she'd go through the windscreen. So he was out.

No 3. Alan; divorced, with two cheeky lads and a ferret. He'd been having problems with his plughole, the house was filthy and he was 'between jobs'. Beverley said she hates ferrets so he was out.

No 4. Timothy; good looking, own house, doting mother designer clothes, a big moustache and a degree in English literature. The house was full of books, he said he liked Kipling. She said he can kipple on his own, I'm not into that sort of thing.

So It's down to Horace, but he said that he owes a lot of money on his bank card. I think he's trying to tell her something.
Beverley said Horace keeps trying to get her into the bedroom. She's told him she's quite comfortable in the lounge. She asked him could she watch Crimewatch, 'cos she'd read in The Chorley Guardian there were men who were trying to take advantage of women through dating agencies, and she doesn't want to be one of them.
I'm meeting Beverley in the pub tomorrow, and looking forward to the next episode.

Joan Patrick is a retired nurse and farmer's wife. Amongst her many activities she shows Lancashire Heeler dogs and writes humorous dialect poetry.

POETRY CAN BE BAD FOR YOUR HEALTH
by Margot Agnew

There's a lot of talk these days about stressful occupations and workers needing counselling but I bet none of you have ever considered the dangers of poetry. Yes – that's right – poetry; it can cause you untold stress and threaten both your job and lifestyle.

Look what happened to the Archbishop of Canterbury. There he was, living a modest life as Bishop of Wales, quite happy with his day job, and like the rest of us, penning a few poems on the side which he published in the church magazine. Of course he wrote the poems in Welsh, just to show how clever he is, but most people didn't have a clue what he was writing about – except for a tiny ethnic minority – the Druids.

Well these Druids said that's the man for us, we'll offer him the Bardic throne for poetry and maybe he'll bring along a few of his mates to join our circle and then we can increase the subscription rate. Now the Bish is delighted that a couple of people can read his poems and understand them, so he says I'd love to join your circle and take the throne; after all I'm a Bishop, I'm used to sitting on thrones.

So at the Druids annual bash, they crown the Bish King of the Poets and because he's a Bishop and a big name in Wales (even if the rest of us haven't heard of him) they get the TV cameras down to record the event. The result is that the Bish makes News at Ten getting crowned by the Chief Druid.

Now if that had been you or me, we'd have been thrilled and put it on our CV. I expect the Bish bragged about it to his mates as well.

Sometime after this crowning event, the Bish gets promoted to Archbish of Canterbury, which makes a lot of people jealous. Especially the Evangelicals, the Calvinists and the Reformists because their man didn't get the job.

These Christian men convocate their holy forces and seek divine inspiration to dethrone the Archbish, get him properly booted out and the job passed on to one of their mates. Unfortunately there's not much in the Archbish's background to rake over – no dodgy liaisons with choirboys, no secreting church funds in suspect off-shore securities, none of that sort of thing, *then they come to the poetry.* Here's where the Archbish has really blown it – on TV for all the world to see, taking part in A Pagan Ceremony.

The Evangelicals, the Calvinists and the Reformists immediately declare the Archbish a Heretic. What a conundrum; the top man in the Church of England a Heretic. A terrific row breaks out, with these guys insisting that the Archbish resign. I was quite disappointed at that, but I suppose burning at the stake has been repealed under the Human Rights Act.

Of course the press seized on the story and doorstepped the Archbish – Hello Archbish, how does it feel to be branded a heretic? – that sort of thing. The poor man had to lie low whilst his religious credibility took a bashing.

Now none of this would have happened if the Archbish had joined Chorley Writer's Circle instead of the Druid's circle. We meet on the fourth Tuesday of every month and offer all kinds of advice to writers. We would have told the Archbish that doing a deal with the Druids was incompatible with Christianity – a bit like vanity publishing really, the price is too high for the small gains. So come along at 7.30pm to Astley Hall Farmhouse; we welcome everybody, even Welsh Bishops.

Margot Agnew is Secretary of Chorley and District Writers Circle and a member of the Publications Committee at Commonword. She writes short stories, novels and plays.

THE LAST WORD
by Carol Thistlethwaite

On behalf of Chorley and District Writers' Circle I would like to say a huge thank you to our sub-committee: **Margot Agnew, Glenda Charlesworth, Liz Perry** and **Gwen Weiss.** They gave the planning, commitment and energy that made our 3 month writing festival, All Write, the success it was.

Participants ranged from those who were beginning to consider taking up writing as a pastime to published writers. The workshops were successful in developing and inspiring people of all abilities. I hope you enjoyed reading this anthology which is a collection of some of the work produced as a direct result of All Write.

Carol Thistlethwaite is the Chairperson of Chorley and District Writers Circle